This book
belongs to

....

Muddle
The Magic Puppy

TOYSHOP TROUBLE

Muddle

The Magic Puppy

TOYSHOP TROUBLE

by Hayley Daze

Willow
Tree

This edition published by Willow Tree Books, 2018
Willow Tree Books, Tide Mill Way, Woodbridge, Suffolk, IP12 1AP
First published by Ladybird Books Ltd.

0 2 4 6 8 9 7 5 3 1

Series created by Working Partners Limited,
London, WC1X 9HH
Text © 2018 Working Partners
Cover illustration © 2018 Willow Tree Books
Interior illustrations © 2018 Willow Tree Books

Special thanks to Jane Clarke

Willow Tree Books and associated logos are trademarks and/or
registered trademarks of Tide Mill Media Ltd

ISBN: 978-1-78700-458-0
Printed and bound in Great Britain
by Bell and Bain Ltd, Glasgow

www.willowtreebooks.net

For Eric and Janice,
great friends and neighbors

When clouds fill the sky and rain starts to fall,
Ruby and Harry are not sad at all.
They know that when puddles appear on the ground,
A magical puppy will soon be around!

Muddle's his name, he's the one
Who can lead you to worlds of adventure and fun!
He may be quite naughty, but he's clever too,
So come follow Muddle—he's waiting for you!

Contents

Chapter One
Amazing Discoveries

"Look at all these toys!" Ruby gasped.
She and her cousin Harry were in
Grandpa's living room, peering inside
an old toy chest. Ruby could see a
jumble of model trains and airplanes,
marbles, and motorcars. They were the
toys Grandpa had played with when he

was a little boy.

"What do you think that is?" Harry asked, pushing his glasses up the bridge of his nose and pointing to a gleaming red-and-green object.

"Let's have a look," Ruby said, leaning so far into the toy chest that only her feet were sticking out. She moved aside a big wooden truck, a tank, and some small metal cars that got tangled in her long braids. Then she grabbed the green-and-red toy and passed it to Harry.

"It's a clockwork train," Harry said, his eyes shining. At the front of the train was the engine, and there were three carriages behind it.

"It's the 2:15 from Grand Central," Ruby said, "and Teddy is going to visit Chips!" Teddy was Ruby's toy duck-billed platypus. He had a long, furry brown body, four big feet, and

a beak like a duck's. Stitched to his bottom was a new pink tail Ruby's mom had sewn on after a tug-of-war accident.

Ruby sat Teddy on one of the carriages and Harry turned the key in the top of the train and set it on the carpet. It moved across the room in the direction of Chips, Harry's toy robot.

"Go, Teddy!" Ruby said.

Tappety, tappety, tap. The train ran into a desk leg and ground to a halt, but the noise of drumming carried on.

Tappety, tappety, tap.

Ruby jumped up in excitement. "It's raining!" she cried, running to look at

the raindrops pitter-pattering against the windows. Ruby could feel bubbles of excitement fizzing up inside her. The last time it rained, a little puppy called Muddle had arrived, and they had all been swept away on an amazing magical adventure!

The back door blew open, hitting the kitchen countertop with a bang. A bundle of fur zoomed into the room like a rocket, knocked over the clockwork train, Chips and Teddy, and leaped into the toy box. It landed—plumpf—on the toys inside.

"Muddle!" Ruby shouted, clapping her hands with delight.

Ruby and Harry looked inside the

toy box to see a little puppy staring back at them. His pink tongue was lolling out and his tail wagged happily.

Harry patted Muddle on the head. "I'd forgotten what a naughty puppy he is."

"He's pretending to be a toy!" Ruby

said, laughing. She scooped him up in her arms. "He's definitely as cuddly as Teddy."

"Woof! Woof!" barked Muddle, as if he agreed. Then he wriggled free, dashed across the room, through the kitchen, and into the rainy backyard.

"Come on!" Ruby shouted with excitement. They rushed after him.

Outside, Muddle bounded down the path, splashing in the puddles. His tail was wagging so hard that a blur of raindrops sprayed out. Ruby held out her hands to catch some of the sparkling drops. From behind his glasses, Harry's eyes were shining.

Muddle stopped in front of a particularly large pool of water and raced around and around it. The raindrops were making the surface ripple and shimmer. He crouched down, then jumped into the water with a splash—and disappeared right through the puddle. Just like last time.

Muddle

The Magic Puppy

Ruby grinned at Harry. "Are you ready for our next adventure?" she asked.

"We won't know until we try," Ruby said. "One, two, three—JUMP!"

And they leaped into the puddle.

***

Muddle

The Magic Puppy

Chapter Two
The Puppy and the Professor

Ruby found herself in complete darkness, surrounded by soft, fluffy objects.

"Muddle," Ruby called, "where are you?"

Muddle gave a yip.

"I've never seen a Robodog toy

before," said a loud, deep voice. "He looks so amaze-errifically real!"

"What's happening?" Harry whispered from somewhere next to Ruby.

"I don't know," she said, "but we need to get out of here!"

She and Harry wriggled their way upward through the soft objects. Light began to seep through. Ruby pushed aside a cuddly dinosaur—and realized that they were inside a huge toy box. It was even bigger than Grandad's. The toy box was inside a large room with high ceilings. Shelves lined the walls, and they were bursting with every kind of toy Ruby could imagine—

teddy bears, jigsaws, video games, and train sets. Long ladders were fixed to the shelves, and people in red aprons were climbing up them, putting more wonderful toys on display. There was a cash register at the front of the room.

"Look!" Harry pointed to a sign written in enormous sparkly letters, high up on the wall.

"Gigglesworth Toys," Ruby read. "We're inside a huge toy store!"

"And there's Muddle," Harry said, his forehead wrinkled with worry.

The little puppy was tucked under the arm of a tall man in a white lab coat. He was carrying a box with the other arm. "Amaze-eriffic," the man

Muddle
The Magic Puppy

said, looking down at Muddle. "I must find out how to make one of these."

"He thinks Muddle's a toy," Harry gasped.

"We're coming, Muddle!" Ruby called.

She and Harry scrambled out of the enormous toy box. When Muddle saw them, he squirmed out from the man's arm and scampered under his feet— tripping the man over.

Crash! The man's box went flying. All sorts of odds and ends rolled across the floor.

"Oh, no!" the man cried, running his hands through his spiky white hair. Then he looked at Muddle. "You're not a Robodog, are you?"

"Muddle's real," Ruby said, smiling. "He can be rather naughty sometimes. We'll help you tidy up."

Ruby knelt down, gathering the cotton reels, ribbon, string, and shiny buttons that had fallen out of the man's box. Beside her, Harry collected nuts and bolts and an electronic circuit board. Muddle ran to greet Ruby and Harry. When the man patted his head, Muddle dropped a pot of glue by the man's feet.

"You didn't mean to make a mess, did you, Muddle?" said the man. "I'm Professor Toyjoy," he added, shaking Ruby and Harry by the hand

and Muddle by the paw.

"I'm Ruby," Ruby said, "and this
is my cousin, Harry. What are these

things?" she asked the professor as he repacked his box.

"My fixi-mend kit," the professor replied. "I can't get the thing-gummy-bobby to work. Nothing works today!"

"Perhaps we can help fix the thing-gummy-bobby," Harry said, "if you tell us what it is..."

"That's wondrously kind, but thing-gummy-bobbies have to be kept top secret," Professor Toyjoy told them, putting the lid back on the box. "What a day!" he murmured. He looked at his watch. "I have to get to work. Time's zippety-zipping away."

Professor Toyjoy backed hastily through the swing doors at the back of

the toyshop.

Ruby saw that Muddle was nosing at something behind the toy box. "What have you got there?" she wondered, taking the object from Muddle's mouth.

"It's a kind of screwdriver," said Harry. He pressed the button on its end,

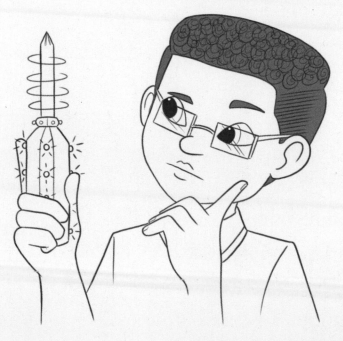

and the screwdriver whirred around.
Red and blue lights flashed on its
handle. "I've never seen one like this
before. It must have fallen out of the
professor's box."

Ruby hurried over to the swing
doors. "We need to find him and give
it back!"

Muddle
The Magic Puppy

Chapter Three
Top Secret Toys

Ruby, Harry, and Muddle pushed through the swing doors and into a long, twisting corridor. It was empty.

"Where's the professor?" Ruby asked.

The corridor was lined with open doors. Ruby and Harry peered inside

the first one and saw two women in white lab coats, sawing out jigsaw pieces.

"They're making toys for the store," Harry whispered.

"Maybe the professor's in one of these rooms," Ruby suggested.

Through each door they saw lots of different sorts of toys—boxed games, video games, toys with batteries, toys with wheels. There was a whole room of airplanes, another of trains and one of princess dolls dressed in pink. In another room, a man was pumping up brightly colored beach balls and stacking them in a neat pyramid.

Muddle wagged his tail and trotted

inside. He batted one of the balls with
his paw, making it bounce around the
room. Ruby ran over and steadied the
wobbling beach ball pyramid.

"We're very sorry," she said to

the man. "Muddle didn't mean to be
naughty—he just wants to play."

But the man was grinning. "That's
what these beach balls are for!" He
tickled Muddle's ears.

"Have you seen Professor Toyjoy?"

Harry asked.

Before the man could reply, Muddle yapped loudly and scampered back into the corridor, his paws pattering against the tiles. Ruby ran out and saw the back of a spiky white head. The professor was walking toward another set of swing doors at the end of the corridor.

"Professor Toyjoy!" Ruby called.

But the professor had already gone through. Above the doors was a sign that said: INVENTORS AT WORK TOP SECRET.

"Do you think we're allowed to go inside?" Harry wondered.

Ruby looked down at the screwdriver in her hand. "The professor won't be able to mend anything if we don't," she said.

Muddle barked his agreement, and pushed the doors open with his nose.

The other side of the doors reminded Ruby of a giant classroom. It was full of men and women in lab coats bent over their workbenches. There were wires and microchips, circuit boards, computer screens, switches, and batteries scattered everywhere.

"It's a laboratory! They must all be toy inventors," Harry whispered, clearly

Muddle

The Magic Puppy

amazed by it all. "I'd like to be an inventor."

Ruby looked around the room. "But where's Professor Toyjoy gone? I can't see..."

But as she spoke, from the back of the workshop there came a bright flash of light and a huge...

...BANG!

Muddle
The Magic Puppy

Chapter Four
The Supertronic Starblaster

Harry and Ruby ducked under the closest bench as a shower of sparkly silver dust rained down on the workshop. Muddle hid his eyes with his paws.

"Professor Toyjoy's exploding things again," a woman said, wiping glitter

from her brow. "At least it's only glitter this time. Last week it was glue, and we were all stuck to the floor."

"Muddle, Harry! Come on!" Ruby scrambled out from under the workbench and raced to the back of the workshop.

The professor was standing in a heap of gently smoking machine parts, shaking his head.

"Dear me," he muttered, rummaging through his fixi-mend kit. "That's the end of the Supertronic Starblaster. And I'll never fix it without my—"

"Is this what you're looking for?" Ruby asked him. She leaped over a pool of silver goo and held out the screwdriver.

"Gracious me!" the professor said, beaming at them. "Thank you!" But then his smile faded as he looked at his watch.

"Is something the matter?" Ruby

asked him. Muddle slithered about in the silver goo and pattered silvery paw prints across the floor.

"I'm just a bit flusterous," he said, running his hands through his hair. "Mr Gigglesworth will be here soon to judge the competition."

"What competition?" Harry asked, prodding what looked like a heap of crumpled-up aluminum foil that had been grilled on a barbecue. Muddle growled as it fell over.

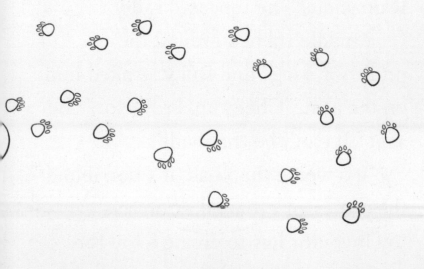

"Mr Gigglesworth's competition," Professor Toyjoy told them. "The competition to find a new bestselling toy for Gigglesworth Toys." He sighed. "The Supertronic Starblaster was my best hope. I designed it to shoot glitteroid stars to stick on children's bedroom ceilings. But it blasted itself, and now everything is ruinacious. Ruinacious!" he repeated sadly.

Muddle rubbed around the professor's legs and Ruby stroked him on the arm. "Cheer up, Professor," she said. "It can't be that bad!"

"It's worse than bad, it's horribloid!" the professor groaned. "You see, every toy inventor has to create a toy for

Mr Gigglesworth's competition.
And these days, all that kids want are
computer gadgets and thing-gummy-
bobbies with batteries..."

"Like my robot, Chips," Harry
agreed.

Professor Toyjoy nodded, then
pointed to his workbench. It was
covered in a red cloth that was draped
over strange lumps and bumps and
sprinkled with silver glitter.

"I've got some fantabulous thing-
gummy-bobbies under there," the
professor said, "but none of them work."
The professor sat down on his chair
and put his head in his hands. "I've
been inventing toys for forty years," he

mumbled. "I don't want to lose my job. It's the most marvel-tastic job-erino in the world!"

Muddle jumped up on his lap and nudged him sympathetically with his nose.

Ruby looked at Harry. He nodded, as if he knew exactly what she was thinking. "Let's help!" she exclaimed.

Chapter Five
Toy Trouble

"Woof! Woof!" Muddle pulled off
the red cloth covering the professor's
workbench. Glitter settled like snow
as Ruby rolled up her sleeves. Under
the red cloth was a jumble of peculiar-
looking toys.

Harry picked up a toy snowman

with an upside-down head. "What are these things?" Harry asked Professor Toyjoy.

The professor looked up. "These watcha-ma-bits? They're all floppers," he sighed, absent-mindedly stroking Muddle's soft ears. "Toys that didn't work."

"Maybe we can help fix one of them," Ruby said eagerly. "Harry's good at fixing things, and I've got lots of ideas."

"I suppose it's worth a try," Professor Toyjoy said. Muddle jumped to the floor as the professor got to his feet and picked up a toy from his workbench. "How about this one—the Whopping

Whale Everlasting Bubble Maker," the professor said, pointing to a basketball-sized machine, shaped like a whale with an open mouth.

"What's wrong with it?" Ruby asked.

"I designed it so the everlasting bubbles can be used as balls," Professor Toyjoy said, pouring a cupful of what looked like bright green slime into the whale's mouth. "But the bubble mix is a bit unrightful..."

They watched open-mouthed as bright green bubbles the size of tennis balls shot out of the whale's blowhole. Muddle jumped up and caught one.

Pop! Muddle yelped with surprise. His nose was splattered with green goo.

Pop! Pop! Pop! Ruby jumped out of the way as the other bubbles burst, spattering green slime everywhere.

"Yuck!" Harry wiped the sticky green ooze off his glasses. "I'd need to look at my chemistry books to help you get that mix right. We don't have time for that right now."

Ruby pointed to something that lookcd like a plastic toy cat sitting on top of a clay machine.

"Perhaps we can make this toy work," she said hopefully.

"It's a Copy Cat," Professor Toyjoy explained enthusiastically. "You put different-colored clay in the machine, and scan your favorite toy with the scantastic scanner, then the Copy Cat computer gadget tells the machine to make an exact copy of the toy."

"Then you can have twice as much fun!" Harry said.

"That's the idea." The professor sighed. "But it isn't quite correctish yet..." He switched on the Copy Cat and handed what looked like a TV remote to Ruby.

"Let's try it!" Ruby said, running

the scanner over the Whopping Whale
Everlasting Bubble Maker.

A multicolored clay snake oozed out
of the machine.

"Grrrr!" Muddle growled, grabbing
the snake and wrestling with it under
the workbench.

Ruby giggled. "These are all

fabulous watcha-ma-bobbies!" she told
the professor.

"But we don't have time to repair-
inate them!" Professor Toyjoy groaned.

"Then we'll just have to invent
something new!" Ruby said.

Muddle

The Magic Puppy

Chapter Six
The Amaze-errific New Toy

Ruby closed her eyes tight and screwed up her face in concentration. What new toy could they invent?

"Woof! Woof! Woof!"

"Muddle!" Ruby cried. "What's the matter?" She opened her eyes and looked around for the puppy.

He was in the corner of the workshop, right next to an old toy chest. She hurried over, closely followed by Harry and Professor Toyjoy.

Muddle was scratching at the

wooden box, as if he was trying to dig his way into it.

Harry shook his head. "Don't be naughty, Muddle," he said.

"I don't think he's being naughty,"

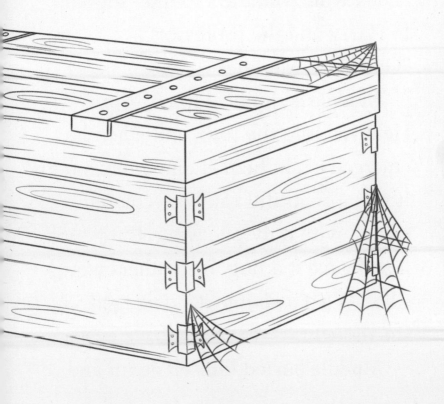

Ruby said. "He wants us to look inside."

Muddle wagged his tail as Ruby lifted the lid.

"Ooh!" Ruby gasped in delight. The box was full of lovely soft toys. "Look what Muddle's found," she said to Harry and the professor. "Good boy, Muddle!"

Muddle scrambled into the box. He dived into the toys, and when he emerged again he had one in his mouth. It was a beautiful rainbow-colored parrot, with only one wing. Ruby took it and gave it a hug. Its feathers were silky. *What a shame it's damaged,* she thought.

Muddle buried himself again and

passed Ruby more toys. There was a friendly-looking furry red dragon that was missing a tail, a plump velvety rabbit without any ears and a yellow-and-black stripy bee with an unstuffed tummy and no antennae. Ruby cuddled each one as he pulled them out. They all looked brand new.

"What's at the bottom, Muddle?" she asked.

Ruby dived head first into the box. She felt around in the darkness. The bottom of the chest was littered with the missing pieces. She stood up clutching them in her arms.

"Don't bother with those old-fangled things," Professor Toyjoy said. "They're

unfinished try-it-outs. When I first
came to work for Gigglesworth Toys,
I designed soft toys. That's not the
sort of thing Mr Gigglesworth wants
now, even if they are splendiferously
cuddleful."

"Splendiferously cuddleful," Ruby
repeated. She thought of Teddy, her
duck-billed platypus, with his pink tail,
duck's beak, and big feet...

Ruby's braids swung as she whirled
around. "I've got an idea!" she squealed.
Soft toys pattered onto the floor as
she climbed out of the toy box. "We
can use these parts to make a new
toy. If everyone else is making gadgets
and video games, a strange and

wonderful cuddly toy is sure to stand out."

"An entirely new crazy cuddly creature..." Harry said slowly. "It might just work."

"That's its name!" Ruby exclaimed excitedly. "Crazy Cuddly Creature!"

Muddle yapped and wagged his tail. "See, Muddle agrees!"

The professor beamed at them. "So do I. That sounds superfantastical!" He turned to Muddle and patted his head. "Go on, Muddle," he said. "Fetch the pieces!"

Muddle leaped back into the toy chest and rummaged enthusiastically through the try-it-out toys. He emerged with a round, purple shape and passed it to Ruby.

"This can be the toy's head," she decided.

Muddle dived back into the toy chest and reappeared with two long, colorful, fuzzy sticks.

"And these are its antennae," Harry said.

Professor Toyjoy clapped his hands. "Now, where's my screwdriver?"

Muddle pulled more pieces from the toy chest, and Ruby and Harry decided what part of the toy each piece would be, holding them in place while Professor Toyjoy fitted their cuddly creation together.

In no time at all, the creature was nearly finished. Ruby thought it looked amaze-eriffic. It was the size of a big teddy bear, and as well as its antennae, it had bright blue buttons for eyes, rabbit ears and whiskers on its nose, parrot's wings, a dragon's tail and feet,

and a fat bee-striped tummy. It even
had a pouch on its front that held a
little bear.

Ruby just couldn't help smiling when she looked at it. It was a perfect Crazy Cuddly Creature.

"Mr Gigglesworth is in the toy store!" a loudspeaker announced, just as Professor Toyjoy finished attaching the creature's tail. "Toymakers! It's time to present your toys!"

Chapter Seven
Competition Time

Muddle's furry head poked out of the toy chest. He had a long blue ribbon in his mouth.

"Well done, Muddle," Ruby said. "That's the finishing touch." She quickly tied a colorful bow around the Crazy Cuddly Creature's neck and

thrust it into Professor Toyjoy's arms. She tugged on her braids for luck and wished as hard as she could that Mr Gigglesworth would like the Crazy Cuddly Creature as much as she did.

All around them, the other toy inventors were scurrying to grab their whizzing, bleeping creations and line up in front of their workbenches. Professor Toyjoy regarded them with dismay.

"Oh dear me," he groaned. "Look at all those whizz-bang inventions. I can't show Mr Gigglesworth a soft toy. It doesn't *do* anything."

Ruby and Harry looked at each other in horror as Mr Toyjoy pushed

the Crazy Cuddly Creature into the toy chest. Only its antennae were left sticking out. Muddle whined and nipped at the antennae.

Before Ruby and Harry could do anything, a tall, skinny man wearing a hat and a suit entered the workshop. He was holding the hand of a very bored-looking boy.

A murmur of excitement rippled through the room. Mr Gigglesworth had arrived!

The boy yawned.

"Who is he?" Ruby whispered.

"That's Mr Gigglesworth's grandson, Max," Professor Toyjoy whispered. "He gets to play with every

toy that's ever made."

"He doesn't look very happy about it," Ruby said. "I'd love to play with every toy that's ever been made."

"You'd soon get bored if playing

with toys was your job," Harry told her,
"like Max."

"Boredomification is always a
problem," Professor Toyjoy muttered.
"In order for a toy to win, Max has to
like it, and he's very hard to please."

I'd never get bored with toys, Ruby
thought, and imagined herself floating
in a toy box boat in a sea of toys.

Mr Gigglesworth made his way
through the workshop with a very
serious look on his face. He stopped
for a few seconds in front of each new
toy, and either nodded or shook his
head and frowned. Max shuffled along
behind him, yawning and shrugging his
shoulders, hardly bothering to glance at

each new invention.

Mr Gigglesworth stopped in front of the professor's workbench. "Professor Toyjoy, where is your new toy?" he asked.

"Oh dear me," Professor Toyjoy sighed sadly. "None of my toys were fantastical enough to present to you today. I fear my toy-making days are over."

The workshop fell silent.

The other toy inventors were staring at
Professor Toyjoy.

"Woof! Woof! Woof!" Muddle
grabbed the Crazy Cuddly Creature's
antennae. The little puppy struggled
to pull the toy out. The toy was bigger
than he was, but he just about managed

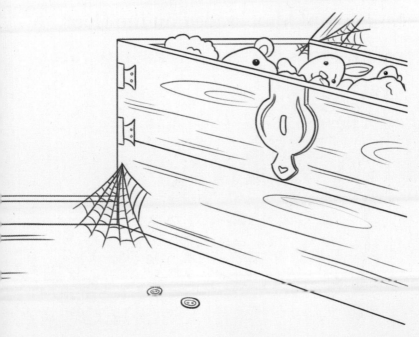

to drag it across the workshop floor.

"Oh, you naughty puppy—come back!" Ruby cried. She tried to catch hold of Muddle, but missed. She staggered to her feet as the puppy hurled himself at Mr Gigglesworth's grandson, Max.

Thump! Max landed on the floor

with Muddle and the Crazy Cuddly
Creature on top of him.

"I am so very full of sorryness,
Mr Gigglesworth!" Professor Toyjoy
exclaimed. "I think we had better leave
now. Goodbye." The professor hurriedly
ushered Ruby, Harry, and Muddle
toward the workshop door.

"Not so fast!" Mr Gigglesworth
thundered. "Come back here!"

Muddle put his tail between his legs
and whimpered.

"Oh dear, Muddle," Ruby said.
"You've got us in real trouble now!"

Chapter Eight
Toy Joys

"Just look what you've done to my grandson!" Mr Gigglesworth boomed.

Ruby, Harry, Muddle, and Professor Toyjoy turned around slowly. Muddle stood behind Ruby's legs. Ruby was afraid of what she might see.

Max was sitting up, hugging the

Crazy Cuddly Creature, with a huge smile across his face.

Ruby's mouth dropped open. So did Harry's and the professor's. Muddle's ears pricked up and his tail started to

wag. He ran over to give Max's cheek a big lick.

Mr Gigglesworth's severe face suddenly softened and his eyes twinkled. "I can hardly believe it!" he gasped. "I've never seen a toy make Max smile before. He loves it!"

Mr Gigglesworth turned to the other toy inventors.

"I hereby declare Professor Toyjoy's creation the winner of the Gigglesworth Toys Competition!" he announced. The other inventors clapped and cheered.

"It's a marvel-fabulo-terrific-acious toy!" Max declared, holding the Crazy Cuddly Creature like a toy airplane, and swooping it around his head.

Muddle
The Magic Puppy

"It can be anything I want it to be. Watch out for the skydiver!"

Mr Gigglesworth caught the little teddy bear as it flew out of the creature's pouch. He and his grandson were both smiling from ear to ear.

"Hip, hip, hooray!" Ruby and Harry cheered as Mr Gigglesworth came over to shake the professor by the hand.

"Yip! Yip! Yip!" Muddle wagged his tail so hard that his whole body waggled.

"What a flabbergastic day!" Professor Toyjoy beamed at Ruby and Harry. "I simply can't thank you enough for your help." Muddle's tail bumped against his legs, and the

professor stroked his ears. "And you, Professor Muddle," he added. "You're a proper toy inventor!"

They all laughed, then Muddle tugged at the hem of Ruby's dress.

"Is it time to go home, Muddle?" she asked.

Muddle barked, and started running in circles around Ruby and Harry. The faces around them started to blur as Muddle ran faster and faster.

"Goodbye, Professor Toyjoy!" Ruby called. "Make lots more Crazy Cuddly Creatures. It'll be a bestseller in the toy store!"

"Absolutifferously!" Professor Toyjoy replied, waving them goodbye.

Muddle
The Magic Puppy

Gigglesworth Toys seemed to melt away, and Ruby closed her eyes...

***

When Ruby opened her eyes again, she, Harry, and Muddle were sitting on a picnic blanket next to Grandpa's toy

box. It was laid out with plates of fruit and sandwiches and glasses of old-fashioned lemonade. Teddy and Chips were already seated.

"I'm back, Teddy!" Ruby cried, giving her duck-billed platypus a hug.

Harry switched on his robot and its eyes flashed.

Muddle ran across the picnic blanket, licked Ruby's and Harry's faces, and ran outside. Ruby and Harry ran to the window to watch him, but the little puppy had already disappeared.

Ruby bent down to pick something up from the doormat. "It's the little teddy from the Crazy Cuddly Creature's pouch," she said, showing it to Harry.

"I can't wait for our next adventure with Muddle," Harry said.

Ruby smiled at her cousin. "Me too. I hope it rains again soon!"

Muddle
The Magic Puppy

Can't wait to find out
what Muddle will do next?
Then read on! Here is the first
chapter from Muddle's third
story, Ballet Show Mischief...

Muddle
The Magic Puppy

BALLET SHOW MISCHIEF

"Ladies and gentlemen, the show is about to begin!" Ruby shouted from behind the plush red bedspread hanging across Grandpa's living room. She closed her eyes for a moment and imagined a huge theater filled with people, calling her name.

"Ruby! Ruby!"

She waved to her imaginary fans, until she realized they sounded like her cousin Harry.

"Ruby! Ruby, can you hear me? What are you doing back there?"

he asked.

"It's a surprise." She giggled, and peeked around the bedspread. "Ready?"

"Um, sorry, Ruby, I've got to finish this maze," Harry said, pushing his glasses back in place, and burying his nose in a puzzle book.

Never mind, Ruby thought as she
ducked back behind the curtain, the
show must go on. She took a big breath
and tugged on her braids for luck. Her
stomach felt as if it was being tickled
by fairy wings. She pulled back her
pretend curtain.

"Welcome to Ruby's Enchanted
Ballet," she said, holding the edges
of her wrinkly tutu and curtsying
like she'd seen real dancers do.
The wall behind Ruby was covered
with drawings of rainbows, castles,
mountains and forests. Ruby had
colored them all in herself, on separate
sheets of paper, and taped them
together.

She twirled around on her tiptoes
with her arms high above her head.
But her stripy tights were slippery.
Her legs slid in opposite directions,
causing Ruby to accidentally do the
splits. "Ta da!" she sang with her arms
outstretched, turning the splits into a
part of her dance routine.

"So that's what you've been working
on all morning," Harry said and closed
his puzzle book.

Ruby pushed the "play" button on
Grandpa's music player and soft violin
music filled the air.

"Now watch me do a spinning top,"
she said, holding out her tutu and
twirling to the music.

"Those are called pirouettes," Harry corrected her, "but I think you hold your arms out like this." He got up from his chair and spun around on his toes with his arms curved in front of him, using them to help him whirl around. "Woah, that really makes you dizzy," he said, sitting down again.

"And this is my graceful swan," Ruby said. She balanced on one foot and stuck out her arms like wings.

"The real name for that is an arabesque," Harry said.

"I like my name better," Ruby replied, still on one foot. "How come you know so much about ballet?"

"My parents love watching ballet at

Muddle
The Magic Puppy

the theater, and sometimes they make me go too," Harry said.

Just then the wind blew the front door open with a BANG! Ruby's pictures were whipped from the wall. They swirled around the living room and finally fluttered to the floor.

A puppy dashed onto Ruby's stage and shook himself, spraying water

everywhere.

"Muddle!" shouted Ruby, twirling on her toes in delight.

Every time it rained, Muddle the naughty little puppy appeared, and swept Ruby and Harry off on a magical adventure.

"Now that's what I call an entrance," Harry said with a laugh.

Muddle tugged at the curtain until it was closed.

"I guess that means my show is over," Ruby said, taking a sweeping bow.

"But our fun has only just begun!" Harry said, chasing Muddle out into the rain.

To be continued...